Mrs. Freedle's High Seas Adventure

K.R. BURG

Illustrations by Martha Hekman

ISBN: 0997204028
ISBN-13: 9780997204025

Illustrations by Martha Hekman

Book design by Publish Pros
www.publishpros.com

Dedicated to all the teachers
who teach right up to recess time
and to all the books
waiting patiently to be read.

There once was a teacher
named Mrs. Freedle.
Mrs. Freedle liked to
sip a nice lemonade
or swing on a swing
or read a good book.

Sometimes, Mrs. Freedle did all three
at the same time.

Most of all,
Mrs. Freedle loved
reading books.

Big books, small books
books with circles, books with colors
and squiggly lines
or pages and pages
of animals
and heroes.
Books inside of other books
and books that pop out
or take you to far-away lands
and sing songs
or books with nothing fancy at all.

One day,
the students in Mrs. Freedle's class
couldn't wait to play
at recess time.

There was just one problem:
it wasn't recess time yet.

Mrs. Freedle knew just
what to do.

"It's time for a story!"
she announced and
gathered the students.

"Anytime you open a book
you go on an adventure,"
Mrs. Freedle said
as she turned
to the first page.

"There once was a
princess who lived
by the sea,"
Mrs. Freedle read
as the students
quieted down.

One day
a great, big ship
came to the land.

The princess
was invited to
board the ship.

Once aboard the ship
the princess was
given chores:
to cook
and clean,
and
scrub the deck.

But the princess
said, "No!
I am a princess!
I don't know how
to cook and clean."

"Then you must
walk the plank!"
the captain said.

The princess walked
to the edge of the plank
and looked down below.

The waters below
were very,
very,
very
dangerous.

Suddenly,
a band of brave heroes
swooped in
and
chased the pirates
away!

"My heroes!"
the princess cried.
"Thank you
for saving me!"

"Thanks to the
band of heroes,
the princess lived
happily-ever after,"
Mrs. Freedle said
as she closed the book.

Just then,
the recess bell rang.

Made in the USA
Lexington, KY
17 November 2018